Sen & Skylen

HOLIDAYS WITH MY HITTA

Iisha Monet

Skylen

"Sorry I'm late! I had to drop the baby off." I greeted Lauren when I made it over to where she was sitting.

"You don't need to apologize to me. I understand. I ordered you a drink."

"Girl you must have read my mind. I pumped for the rest of the day, so this drink is very much needed."

We were meeting for our weekly lunch date at TGI Friday's, and lord knows I needed this. Ever since I had Sencere my life only consisted of working and being a mother. Don't get me wrong, I love being a mother to my child but it's tough doing it on my own. I never imagine this being my life but it was and there was nothing I could do about it.

"So, how's my god baby?" Lauren asked taking a sip out of the mule she was drinking.

"You would know if you were still at the house."

"Biiitchhhh. Don't go there. You need your own space, and besides, I love my little Sen, but he cries too much!"

"Did you just come for my baby?" I asked her with one of my eyebrows raised.

"Never! You know I would never do that. I'm just saying I can't masturbate in peace without hearing him crying right before a bitch is about to cum."

"Really bitch?"

"You asked hoe." She joked just before our waiter came over to us and took our orders.

"How was your date the other night?" I smiled being nosey.

"It was cool. It was just a date. I don't even know why I even bothered honestly. I keep going out with these men and women all to delete their numbers afterwards. A complete waste."

"Lauren.. You need to pick one. You've been on at least eight dates in the past two weeks."

"I know, but they're all so blah. No personality. No sense of humor. Great jobs and fine as hell but they aren't speaking to my soul. I haven't been wowed yet. I thought one came close. Remember the guy John I went out with last week? Well, we texted for a couple of days, and then he had the audacity to pop up at my condo!"

"Shut up! For real?"

"Yes, girl. Luckily the security wouldn't let him in. I stood there and watched the whole thing. He saw me and tried flagging me down, but I acted like I didn't know him. Dumb ass caused a whole scene." She vented rolling her eyes.

"I was so embarrassed."

"You must've fucked him" I side eyed her, and she ignored me by taking a sip of her almost finished drink.

"Don't ignore me. I know you fucked him miss I date more bitches then men."

"I needed some dick, and he was fine. Don't

judge me!"

"I ain't judging boo. Do ya thang!"

"Whatever. Anywayssss, what's going on with you? Sen still calling?" She inquired, and I rolled my eyes.

Since Sen has been in jail, he has called me faithfully every day and I faithfully never answer. I had nothing to say to him. Yes, we share a child ,but that's about it. I could never forgive him for hurting me. He knew who Leland was so my thing is why kill him? I have so many questions that needed answering, but I refuse to talk to him. Ms. Jenn, his mother, is the only communication the two of us have when it regards our son.

"You know he is. I wish he would fuckin' stop though." I sighed playing with my straw.

"No, you don't. If you did you would either block his calls or change your number. Just admit you still care about him. It's okay. You're human."

"Lauren.. I mean I do still care about him, but I

can't forgive him for what he did. He betrayed me."

"Do you know why he did what he did though?"

"No, and honestly I don't think there's any logical explanation either."

"You don't know that."

"You're really going to sit here and try to justify him killing someone?!?" I whispered with an attitude.

"I'm not sitting here justifying a damn thing. What I am doing though is trying to look at this situation from all sides. Sen, although I don't know him that well doesn't strike me as someone who does things out of malice." She argued back.

"I said what I said, Lauren. Drop it!"

"And I said what I said. He's still the father of your child. The nigga may be behind bars for life, but he deserves to see his child. Now I'll drop it."

"Whatever," I grumbled. I had lost my appetite. I just wanted to go home and go to bed. She had ruined my entire mood.

****

"You're early." Ms. Jenn spoke to me opening the door letting me in.

"I know. I hope you don't mind. I was missing my baby." I confessed walking into her living room and having a seat.

"He's asleep right now. I just have to get his things together."

"It's okay. I kinda need to talk to you about something."

"What's wrong sweetie?"

"Uh.. did Sen ever tell you why he did what he did?"

"No. I never asked. It isn't my business."

"Oh."

"Why?" She questioned taking a seat across from me.

"Just asking."

"Skylen. I'm old, not stupid. What's on your mind? I may be his mother, but I'm also a woman. Talk to me."

"It's nothing."

"Skylen."

"I just want to know why he did it. I don't understand why and now we have a baby together. How am I supposed to act like none of this happened?" I asked with tears filling my eyes.

I was trying to keep it together, but my emotions won. I'm so overwhelmed with the way my life has been turned upside down. I never signed up for any of this. I never wanted this. How did I even find myself in this situation, to begin with? Had his ass never waltzed into my life I wouldn't even be going through this. I was fine before I met him and now here, I was twenty-seven with a fucking child by a man who killed my boyfriend. You hear how crazy this all sounds?

"First of all, what you're going to do is stop feeling sorry for yourself and put your big girl panties on. I'm not condoning anything my son has done, but you have some unfinished business regarding him, and you need to attend to it. Look at you. You're sitting here crying asking me questions you should be asking him." She spoke.

"I can't talk to him."

"You can, and you will. That man has been calling since he's been in there, worried about you. Skylen baby, you gotta talk to him. I know you don't want to, but you have to. Go up there and see him. Do it for Sencere."

"I'm not taking my baby up there!"

"Hold up now, lower your voice. I never said you had to take him with you. You know I have absolutely no problem keeping him if you need me to while you go see him."

"I don't even know if I can bring myself to look at him."

"You won't know unless you try. Now let me go check on my grandbaby. You need to grow up Sky. I know I'm not your momma but I'm his; and that baby's grandmother, you're family now. Handle your shit!" She said checking me before getting up and leaving me in the room alone.

Why is this my life?

Sen

"Aye, you coming to the rec room?" My cellmate asked me.

"Nah, fam I'm straight," I responded laying on my bunk staring at this dingy ass ceiling.

I cursed myself every fuckin day for being in this fuckin' shit hole. Only good thing keepin' a nigga goin' is the fact that mom dukes hired a high-profile lawyer to work on my case and shit was looking good. Come to find out there's a few flaws in the case so a nigga might be getting out. I ain't gon' front I'm banking on being released. I wanted to meet my seed. I also wanted to talk to Sky. I needed to tell her that shit ain't what she thinks it may be.

I missed shorty. I missed the gentleness about her. She was so naive to things, not in a bad way but in an innocent way. I've been with plenty of women, but none like her. She was different. A diamond in the rough. Bitches, where we from, ain't built like her, and that's what drew me to her. Yeah, she was bad and shit, but she had a great mind. A good head on her shoulders. Aside from that, she birthed my seed. We weren't even fuckin around that long, and she got knocked up. Can't tell me she wasn't it for me.

I spoke to my mother the other day, and she was telling me that she felt like Sky still cared. I wanted to believe that, but I couldn't. Not when she refused to answer calls or even come see me. I know I fucked up, but she could at least give me a chance to explain. Well, maybe not explain but at least apologize for hurting her. If she never spoke to me again after I got a chance to say what I needed to say shit would fuck me up a bit, but I'd be cool because she gave me the opportunity to explain. That's all I needed. That and to meet my son.

****

"Lewis, you got a visitor!" The guard yelled to me walking into the cell.

Wiping my eyes, I stood up and stretched before following him. I don't even know when I had managed to doze off, but that's the type of effect Skylen had on me. I ain't want to do shit but be alone. I was cool with some niggas in here, but they were different than me. They were used to this life, I wasn't. I said I'd never end up back here, but Grimey fuck ass did some hoe shit. Speaking on him, if I'm blessed to see the light of day again, I'm murking that bitch ass nigga as soon as I catch him.

Finally making it to the visiting area, I walked over to the assigned window, and I swore I saw a ghost. There she was. She had put on a little weight, but it looked good on her. Her hair pulled up into a bun and a turtleneck it looked like. Her makeup looked perfect, it kinda gave her a glow, and my dick threatened to stiff up. Taking a seat, we just looked at one another. She looked sad. Hurt. Disappointed. All in one and I understood. She had every right to, it just fucked with me that I was the reason she was feeling that way.

I didn't make any moves to grab the phone until I saw her make one. When she did, she just held it to her ear and looked at me. She probably opened her mouth a thousand times before clearing her throat to speak.

"Hey," she said softly, and I realized just how much I missed her voice.

"Sup? You good?" I responded.

"Sen.. I.. Uh.. I've seen better days. You?"

"I'm as good as can be considering the circumstances. How's the baby?"

"Good. He's getting big. He looks like you." She smiled, I'm assuming thinking about him.

"That's wassup," I spoke trying not to be in my feelings about not meeting the child I helped create.

"So wassup Sky? I know you ain't come up here just to look at me. What's on your mind ma?"

"I can't do this!" She quickly said standing up with the phone still to her ear.

"Sit down Skylen. Now!"

"Sen.."

"Sit down. What you want answers?" I asked her already knowing the answer.

Instead of responding she chewed on her bottom lip like she always did when she was nervous. It was a bad habit of hers. She wore her heart on her sleeves and emotions all on her face. She was fighting with herself. She wanted to hate me but that twinkle in her eyes let me know that she loved me, but I had did the unforgivable.

"Sky, we only got thirty minutes to talk, you wasting time. Have a seat."

Listening she took a seat and tears fell from her eyes. I hated seeing women cry. Shit fucked with me but Skylen crying was on a whole different level because I was the cause of those tears. Fucked up part about it is she was crying, and I couldn't do shit to console her.

"Come on Sky, stop crying."

"The whole drive here I imagined how this conversation would go. I told myself I wasn't going to cry, and I was coming here for closure but looking at you I can't help but hate you for doing this to us. You did this Sen! Nobody else. You did! I just want to know why!" She vented wiping her tears with the back of her free hand.

"I didn't mean to hurt you. You have to believe me."

"But you did."

"And I'm aware of that. I can't give you all of the answers you need right now but trust me when I say I didn't know."

"You're lying!"

"I'm not. Look you're upset. I get that but don't ever call me a liar. I'm a lot of things but a liar? Nah wrong nigga baby girl. I fucked up, true indeed but I didn't know. I got a court date coming up in a week. Come. I want you to come and bring the baby. I just want to see him."

"No! Why should I do anything you ask me to do after what you did to me?" She asked being stubborn and slightly irritating me.

Remember when I said she was naive about a lot of things, this is an example. She asking questions that deserved answers but with loopholes being found in my case, you think I'd incriminate myself? Nah. Wrong nigga. I wouldn't even incriminate Grimey like that. He shitted on me, but I would never fold. Ima be a solid muthafucka until I'm six feet under.

"Come to the court date. All of your questions will be answered. Just trust me, aight?"

"I can't do that."

"What you mean you can't do that?" I asked through furrowed eyebrows.

"I can't trust you. Trust is a big word. You don't deserve for me to trust you."

"Skylen, I fucked up ma. I get that, but if I'm telling you to do some shit, it's for your benefit. Just-"

"Lewis time is up!" The guard said loudly.

"Just come ma. I need you." I said standing up

with the phone in my hand.

She didn't even get a chance to respond because I was being escorted away. I needed my lawyer to come through for a nigga. According to him, there was a witness, luckily for me, that witness had disappeared. He didn't know I knew that, but I did. I had already had it taken care of. All the other shit was left up to him to do what the fuck he is being paid to do. I needed to get the fuck up out of here and home to my son.

Skylen

I should have never gone and visited Sen, but noooo I had to listen to his nosey ass momma. Seeing him just made things more conflicted. Seeing him in that jumpsuit did something to me. Granted he still looked good, but I was sad that he was there. Ain't this some shit? I'm feeling sorry for the man who murdered my ex-boyfriend. I sound all types of crazy right now, but it's the truth.

Ever since I made it back home, he was the only thing I could think about. I didn't want to, but I couldn't help it. He looked so sincere. He looked remorseful. I could tell that he didn't mean to hurt me but knowing that he did ate at him; and it should because I really was content with the way things were happening between the both of us. If things didn't happen the way that they did, Sen and I would probably be in a relationship. But since they did there was absolutely no way, we would ever be in one now.

Yes, he's the father of my child, but that's as far as that goes. I know he asked me to make an appearance at his court date, but I wasn't too sure how I felt about all of that. For one Leland's family would be there. For two I have a child by him. That would put me in a weird position.

"Hey, girl hey!" Lauren smiled bright walking into the house before kissing my cheek.

"Hey."

"Eww, what's your problem?"

"I saw Sen."

"You visited him?"

"Nah the nigga facetimed me," I said sarcastically.

"Duh, how else was I supposed to see him?"

"You playing but dudes really be having phones in jail." She said rolling her eyes.

"He in county bitch. He ain't upstate!"

"You right, anyways what happened?"

"He apologized."

"And what else?"

"Damn bitch you thirsty!" I joked laughing.

"Never thirsty hoe, I just want to know what happened because last we spoke you didn't even want to speak to him."

"I went to see him earlier today. I went over to pick Sencere up from Ms. Jenn a couple of days ago, and she suggested I go see him. It was right after the conversation you and I had so I figured I'd go. I fought myself with it, and today I woke up like I'ma just go, so I dropped the baby off with my mom and went up to Ludlow."

"Okayyy but you still not saying nothing. You're still not telling me what happened."

"Nothing happened. He apologized. I asked why he did what he did and he said he couldn't answer for obvious reasons and told me to come to his next court date."

"You going?" She asked leaning over onto the marble counter.

"I don't know. Probably not. He wants me to bring the baby, and I am not tryna have my child around all those germs."

"Yeah, I don't blame you there. But what do you think he wants you to come for?"

"See that's the thing. I don't know. I can't even begin to think of one reason why either."

"You think his momma knows?"

"Of course, she knows. She's team Sen though so she ain't gon tell me shit about her ugly ass son. You know how that is. I went through my shit with Ms. Clara and Leland. She knew all his secrets and still the man could do no wrong. I learned my lesson girl."

"That don't count because Ms. Clara ass is old as hell and shouldn't even have had Leland, to begin with. She babied him and covered up all of his mess. Jenn doesn't strike me as the type. I feel like she wouldn't side with him unless she truly did believe him or something. I can be wrong though so please don't quote me."

"Bitch.. Did you just call that lady old?"

"Am I lying? Ms. Clara remind me of the mother of the church. Old ass egg and old ass sperm produced a dumb ass child. I know I shouldn't be talking ill on the dead, but i can't help it. You know he was not my favorite person." She vented and I just stopped and looked at her.

Something was wrong with this damn girl. She know she ain't have to violate his parents like that. She was wrong as hell for that, but she wasn't lying.

***

"Your honor if you may, I would like to ask for the courts to consider an acquittal due to lack of evidence as well as lack of a witness. I've gone through all documentation, and it has been brought to my attention that both of the witnesses have seemingly disappeared in some form. Which means without any solid evidence or proof by law my client should be released." Some tall white middleaged man spoke.

He was standing next to Sen while Ms. Jenn sat

behind them. Me? I stood in the very back. I wasn't trying to be noticed. Curiosity got the best of me, so I decided to show up like he asked. I didn't feel it was appropriate to bring Senny, so Lauren was looking after him.

After a few more minutes of the lawyer making his point, the judge decided to go for a brief recess. Not even a second later Sen turned around and locked eyes with me. How did he know I was here? How did he know to turn around and look into my direction? For a second, we just looked at one another until I broke eye contact. Adjusting the straps on my purse, I made my exit out of the courtroom.

Judging by the case his lawyer was making, Sen will be coming home soon. Very soon and I wasn't ready for that.

Sen

"I have a really good feeling about this." My lawyer spoke to me taking a seat.

"Oh, yea?" I questioned sitting back in my seat.

"Without any witnesses and solid evidence, they have no choice but to release you or that's a lawsuit waiting to happen. Trust me on this buddy; you'll be a free man today."

"Thank you, Jesus!" My mother smiled.

"When ya black ass gets out you better stay away from that boy, you hear me?"

"Ma."

"Ma hell. You heard me, Jensen. Stay away from him. If they let you off this time, don't do anything to put yourself back into this predicament. You're a father now. Ain't nobody got time for all of this."

"She's right." My lawyer chimed in just as the judge came back out.

"After reviewing both sides of the case, I have

considered an acquittal in favor of the accused defendant. Mr. Lewis, I trust that after you leave my courtroom, you will act like a law-abiding citizen, correct?" The judge spoke looking at me over his glasses.

"Yes. Your honor."

"I don't want to see you back in here. You seem like a decent young man who was wrongly accused. I would hate to see you in here again for the same thing because it will just mean my judgment was wrong. Court is adjourned!"

"I told you."

"Thanks, man. 'Preciate it." I smirked.

"You just stay out of trouble. I'm going to get the paperwork ready for your release. Hopefully, they let you leave from the courthouse. Hang tight. Congratulations!" He told me patting me on my shoulder as the bailiff walked over to me preparing to walk me out.

"Ma Don't start. Fix ya face. I'm cool. I'm coming

home."

"I just don't like how I can't even have a moment with you! I'll be waiting, baby!" She said caressing my cheek before I was led away. Before I made it completely out of the courtroom, I saw a familiar face. She winked before walking away.

***

Stepping out into the cold November air I blew into my hands while I waited on my ride. I didn't get released the day the charges were dropped and the case was dismissed. In fact, it has been an entire week, and a nigga couldn't describe how I was feeling. Ludlow can suck my dick now since I was going home.

"You going to jump in or stand there and catch a cold?" She asked rolling down her window and without hesitation I hopped into the passenger seat.

"Shit clean. When you get this?"

"Couple of weeks ago. I needed something different."

"So, you decided on a truck?"

"Yeah, I had to. I need it for Harmony, you know?" Valencia spoke keeping her eyes on the road.

"How's that been going?" I asked getting comfortable.

"Hard but good. After my aunt died a few months ago, I came back for her. I said I never wanted to step foot into Springfield again, but I had already fucked up so much when it came down to my daughter that I wanted to finally do right by her. Besides, when you hit me up saying you were in a jam, I had to come through and help you. We may not be together but if ever I can help in any way, I will."

"Speaking about that, I appreciate that. I didn't even know you were going to show up at court until I saw you."

"Now you know my nosey ass was coming to that. I had to sneak out before Jenn saw me. You know she don't like me." She joked.

She was different from the last time I saw her. She seemed at peace. She seemed happy. Not the happy she claimed to be when we were together but happy within. She looked like she had got her shit together and that's all I ever wanted from her truthfully. We'll never be together, but I won't front like with the way she's looking I wouldn't fuck because after a year, or so of being locked up, I needed some pussy.

"What's new with you?" I asked looking out the window noticing the leaves falling off of the trees.

"Besides mom life nothing. Just staying out of trouble."

"As you should."

"Sen, I know this is completely off topic, but you need to handle Grimey or let me handle him before I leave town again. He's a rat, so the nigga gotta go."

"I'ma handle it. Don't worry your pretty little self about that. Aight?"

"We might not be together, but I still have love for you. We weren't a good match for each other, but things happened the way that they were supposed to."

"We cool shorty. Leave the past in the past. You

changed. I see it. I'm proud of you. Get up out of here and don't look back. Don't let me and my bullshit suck you back in. I appreciate what you did and shit but move forward. Not backwards." I spoke just as she pulled up to my mother's house and I noticed Skylen's car was parked in front.

"Stay out of trouble Sen. Okay?"

"You already!"

"I'm serious. Stay out of trouble."

"Got you."

"Alright then, take care." She smiled kissing me on the cheek before I got out of her car.

As she pulled off, I remained in the same spot I was standing and just took a couple of deep breaths. I was home. Finally.

Skylen

"Ms. Jenn I got to go. He's getting fussy, and it's time for his nap."

"I just told you he can nap here. You're just in a rush to go home to an empty house!"

Did she just shade me? I feel like she just lowkey called me lonely. I do feel a tad bit lonely from time to time, but I didn't need for her to remind me. This is why I don't come over here unless it has anything to do with Sencere. Other than that, I stay away from Ms. Jenn but she practically begged me to come over today, so here I was annoyed as hell.

"I'm in a rush to go home because-"

"AHHHHH!" She screamed looking behind me causing me to jump and turn around.

I should have known there was a reason for all of her extraness. She knew Sen was coming home. That's why she had cooked a whole bunch of food and was stalling me to keep me from leaving. As I watched them hug one another, he kept his eyes on me as I cradled our son in my arms. After a few moments they broke their embrace, and she turned around to see what had his attention.

"Want to hold him?" I asked.

"He's so little. I don't want to break him."

"You won't break him."

"You see how big I am?" He asked, and I started giggling.

"You won't break him Sen. Here," I told him handing him our son gently.

As angry as I was at him, I couldn't help but get all soft and mushy as I watched him look into Sencere's eyes. Sencere had been fussy the whole time we have been here, and Sen walks in, and he calms down. It's like he knew his daddy was here. The expression I saw on Sen's face kinda reminded me of my own the first time I laid eyes on the baby. We were witnessing perfection in tiny human form. It was an experience in itself.

Instead of harboring over him, I allowed him to bond with his son and walked outside. It was cold out. Glancing over at my old apartment I smiled thinking about the good memories before a small tear escaped my eye. Every time I thought about my life, Leland crossed my mind, and I always felt guilty for having a child with Sen.

I know I can't change what happened. I also don't regret my son because he was meant to be here. I would never question his existence. Not when he's the greatest thing that has happened to me despite everything else. But I still felt I was disrespecting Le's memory. I don't know, maybe I'm just thinking too much. Giving this situation more attention than it needs.

Walking over to my car, I got in and just sat in the driver's seat. I wasn't leaving. I needed to think. I needed to talk to someone. I needed to talk to Lauren, but she was at work so calling her was out of the question. Resting my head on the steering wheel, I closed my eyes briefly until I heard my car door open. It was Sen. I knew it was him without having to look at him. I walked out without saying a word. He was definitely coming to find me, and he did because now we're both sitting in my car in complete silence unsure of what to say to each other.

"Thank you!"

"For what?" I asked him picking my head up looking straight ahead.

"For him. You could have had an abortion."

"I would never do anything like that no matter how much the father may be a fuckboy."

"It's not what you think Sky. I thought I told you that." He countered.

"Then what is it? I keep trying to understand why you did what you did but I keep coming up short!"

"I was paid to do something, so I did. I didn't know it was him."

"So you're a hitman is what you're saying?"

"Nah. I mean I'm not a perfect muthafucka, but I don't go around killing people just for the fuck of it."

"You killed an innocent man Sen. You killed my boyfriend!"

"Ayo! Didn't I say I didn't know it was him? I was paid to do some shit, so I did it. Fuck more you want me to say? You sitting here crying and shit but had no problem fucking me after the nigga was gon' go upside yo head that day. I'm not gon beg you to forgive me ma. I ain't that nigga. I don't kiss ass. All I want is an opportunity to be a father to my child. You can kill this goofy shit." He barked before jumping out of the car and going back into the house.

Instead of following him inside I pulled out my phone and sent Ms. Jenn a text alerting her that I was leaving and Sencere can stay with them for the night. I couldn't be around Sen. I was too distraught to have a conversation with him. Maybe another day we could talk but today? It wasn't happening. It was just a bit too much.

***

"Happy Thanksgiving!" I cheered walking into my parent's home.

"You're early. You getting sick?" My mother asked causing me to laugh.

"I have another stop to make. It's Sencere's first Thanksgiving, and Ms. Jenn insisted that we'd stop by for picture's, so I came here first. Lauren should be coming in at any moment."

"That boy come home?"

"Yes."

"Good, because this child needs a father and can't no man in and out of jail be one."

"Momma!"

"Don't momma me. You heard what I said. He needs a father. You couldn't just go get a decent young man, you had to spread your legs for the heathen!"

"Ma! Really?" I complained sitting the car seat on the sofa just as Lauren walked in.

Everything in my spirit is telling me that my

mother is about to be on some good bullshit. She was too judgmental for my liking which was why I never wanted to tell her about Sen, but I had no choice but to because I couldn't keep lying. I eventually came clean about him being in jail right before the baby shower. She didn't know what he was in for and I prayed that she never did.

It was bad enough I got pregnant out of wedlock. To add to that, I got knocked up by a man I didn't know. Oh, and to add to that, he was a damn criminal, so this conversation my mother is trying to have isn't going to end well. I feel it. With everything that has been going on, I haven't been feeling like myself, and it's only a matter of time before I snap. Unfortunately, today just might be the day that I do.

"What happened?" Lauren asked confused.

"Nothing. Other than my mother insinuating I'm a hoe nothing happened at all."

"Don't put words in my mouth missy! What I said was you couldn't go find a decent man to have sex with instead of a hoodlum? Leland was nice. If you wanted to get pregnant, you should have done that with him." She spoke with an attitude.

"Leland was beating my ass! Does that still make him a nice young man? Huh, momma? Does that make him the poster child for a great father? Because it my memory serves me right, he's dead, and I would still be a single mother!"

"Skylen-"

"No Lauren, I'm so tired of this. Since I got pregnant, it has always been something. I can't do this. I won't do this. Everyone has so much to say but doesn't know the half of what went on!" I spat grabbing my baby's car seat.

"Enjoy your dinner. I'm leaving!"

"Skylen baby wait, I didn't mean it like that. I had no idea." My mother tried calling out, but I ignored her and continued out the door with Sencere.

If it's not one thing, it's another. I was so tired of it. I already felt like shit because I had a child with a man I barely even knew. But I didn't need anyone to make me feel even worse than I already felt. You don't think this situation bothered me? For Christ sakes the nigga killed my ex. You only hear about stuff like this in those damn urban fiction books I be reading.

Making it to the car, I strapped the car seat in before going to get in the driver seat. I was irritated. It's been that way a lot lately. My moods were so up and down — emotions so all over the place. I found myself sometimes sitting in one spot for hours just staring at the walls. I was slowly but surely losing myself. I was spiraling, and I didn't know what to do. Everything triggered me. I needed help. The wannabe psychiatrist needed help.

Sen

"How's things with Skylen?"

"What you mean?" I questioned my mother.

"Y'all get around to talking things out?" She asked stirring up a pot of Collard greens.

"We spoke the day I came home, but that was it if that' what you want to call it."

"You haven't reached out to her since?"

"Nah, I'ma just give her, her space. When she's ready, I guess she'll come around."

"My pitiful child of mine lord. Jensen, you care about the girl, right?"

"Of course, I do."

"Then make her talk to you."

"I'm not gon force myself on no female. If she ain't fuckin' with me, then that's just what it is. I ain't gon beg her though."

"You men are so stupid. Keep playin' around, you hear? She going to end up with someone else. Watch." She spoke rolling her eyes.

"Didn't I tell you to stop categorizing me with all these niggas?" I complained leaning against the door frame.

"Stop acting like them, and I wouldn't have to. You're my son, true indeed but you be doing some stupid shit. I just don't understand it."

"So what am I supposed to be doing since you have all the answers."

"You're supposed to be chasing her. Make her ass talk to you. She cares about you Senny. If she didn't, she wouldn't be so angry with you. She's fighting a battle between what's right and what her heart wants. The whole year you were gone I spent a lot of time with her, and I got to love her like a daughter. She's delicate, and you have to treat her as such. Do something special for her. Show her that you're trying to make an effort. Women like shit like that."

"I hear you."

"Hopefully your arrogant ass is listening to me though." She warned just as the doorbell rang.

"I got it," I told her before making my way to the front door and opening it.

"Your mother invited me." She sniffled, and I grabbed the baby out of her arms before stepping to the side and letting her in.

"You aight?"

"Mmmhmm."

"You're lying but aight."

"It's almost his feeding time; I'll take him." She said reaching for him, but I didn't release him. Instead, I walked towards the kitchen where my mother was now looking at us with her hands on her hips.

"Hey Ms. Jenn"

"Hey baby, I wish you'd stop calling me that, making me feel like an old ass lady!" She fussed.

"It's out of habit." She smiled.

"I invited Lauren, do you mind if she comes by?"

"Not at all. We ain't gonna eat all this food no way."

"It smells good in here."

"Of course, it does because I been bustin my ass in this kitchen all day. I wasn't expecting you for another hour or so. What brings you by so early?"

"I don't want to talk about it. Family drama." She sighed.

"Sen I really gotta feed him."

"So get his bottle ready." I sternly responded, and she looked at me like I was crazy.

"What?"

"I breastfeed. I can't just make him a bottle."

"Sen carry the baby upstairs. Skylen go feed my fat man." Mom duke told us, and we did.

Once we made it to the spare bedroom which was now a room for the baby, Skylen sat down in the rocking chair in the corner before pulling one of her breasts out. Handing our son to her, I watched as he immediately latched on. The sight before me was amazing. She looked so beautiful sitting there nourishing our child. Aside from the stress that was written all over her face, she was stunning.

"You sure you're aight?" I asked taking a seat on the footrest to the chair.

"Yeah, I'm cool."

"Sky, you don't have to lie to me ma. It's me you're talkin' to. What's going on?"

"I'm just so conflicted." She sighed.

"I want to hate you, but I can't because you gave me my greatest gift in life. Still, despite that, a part of me feels betrayed by you and doesn't know whether or not to let my guards down. Meanwhile, the other part can't help but be drawn to you. You got me falling out with my momma and everything. I don't.. I just don't know." She confessed never looking at me.

"What you mean you falling out with ya moms?"

"Nothing. Don't worry about it."

"Nah. Talk to me." I tried egging her on.

This was the most I've been able to get out of her. She was so hell bent on not talking to me that I almost forgot how soft her voice was. Every time she spoke it sounded like the sweetest thing, I ever heard which was rare. I wasn't used to a chick like her. Like I said before she has an innocence about herself and I couldn't help but be drawn to that.

"It's nothing. Don't worry about it."

"Why do you keep doing that? I'm tryna talk to you. I'm tryna be there for you but you ain't fucking with me. I keep telling you I never meant for things to happen like that. You don't trust me?"

"I don't know!" She yelled making Sencere cry.

"Shhhhh, I'm sorry. Mommy's sorry." She chanted rocking him still with her breast in his mouth.

"Look, I can't change what happened. Even if I could, I wouldn't because who knows what would have happened between the two of us. I can't tell you to get over shit, but I can hope that eventually, you find it in your heart to forgive a nigga because my intentions weren't to hurt you. You gotta believe me."

"Sen.. I just need time, okay? I need time to process everything."

"Say no more," I told her before standing up preparing to walk out of the room.

"Wait.. Just because I'm unsure of my feelings for you doesn't mean that I'd stop you from being a father. He's just as much your son as he is mine and I never want to come in between you building a bond with him. He didn't ask to be here, and it isn't his fault that we've found ourselves in this situation."

"I'd never let anything stand in the way of being a father. I didn't grow up with one, so I plan on doing things differently. I appreciate you for saying that though." I told her placing a kiss on her forehead and leaving her to be alone.

Skylen had me fucked up. Like mentally I wasn't too sure what to say or do with her so if time is what she needed, then time is what I'll give her.

Skylen

It had been a few days since Thanksgiving, and I still wasn't speaking to my mother. I had nothing to say to her until she apologized. She was rude for her comments, and until she owned up to that, her and I weren't speaking. I felt judged, and that's what I never wanted. I may not have had done what she would have, but that doesn't give her the right to just judge me like she was perfect.

With Sencere laying down taking a nap, I busied myself with cleaning. I always cleaned when I found myself stressed out. I wasn't stressed about anything major, it was Sen. I so desperately wanted to be around him, yet I couldn't bring myself to tell him that.

Being around him sparked those old feelings I used to get whenever we were around each other. I felt like I was crushing and lusting all over again. I just was unsure on what to do. I feel like if the universe didn't want us together then why would it make us parents to a child we shared. Why would we both still be very much attracted to each other as we have been from the very beginning. I wasn't understanding it, and maybe it wasn't for me to understand, yet I still tried to anyways.

Taking a seat on my sectional, I pulled out my iPhone and facetimed Lauren. After stopping by Ms. Jenn's house on Thanksgiving her and I haven't really spoken much, and I missed my girl. I hadn't even gotten a chance to tell her about Sen and I last conversation. After a few rings, she answered sitting in the bathtub.

"What you want heffa? You're interrupting my me time."

"If you were having me time why would you answer? Does that make any sense to you?"

"Well, bitch I saw your name and answered. Something could have been wrong with our baby."

"The baby is fine. I wanted to talk to you."

"About?" she questioned putting a glass of wine

to her lips and drinking it.

"I know your ass don't have wine while you're taking a damn bath."

"Don't worry about what I'm doing. What's up?"

"I can't stand you! Anyways I never told you that I spoke to Sen on Thanksgiving."

"I mean I figured you had spoken to him because you weren't being a total bitch to him." She sassed.

"You think you know me so well, huh?" I questioned with a giggle.

"Not at all but you two weren't hostile to one another, so I figured y'all were cool."

"That's the thing no matter what he's never hostile to me. He doesn't get disrespectful. He may get upset or whatever, but he never really argues with me which is odd because I know he has it in him."

"That's because he cares about you."

"You think so?"

"I know so. I knew after the moment he beat you

know who ass, for you without knowing you. Y'all had a connection from the very beginning. I noticed that day we were at Chilli's. You remember that day?" She asked, and I did.

It was a day we went to lunch, and he walked in with Valencia. My little ol' heart was crushed when I realized they were dating but at that time I had no room to be because we didn't know each other. He had just helped out with my tire, and we spoke briefly at Center Stage.

"That doesn't mean anything." I tried brushing it off.

"It means a lot. The man ain't perfect Sky, but he's perfect for you. You just have to open your pretty brown eyes wide and realize that. Not saying forget what he did but I honestly think you should consider forgiving him."

"It's not that simple though Laur. You know that. If Le was just a dude I was fucking with I wouldn't care but he's not. He's a dude I spent years with. Damn near a decade. I can't help but feel some sort of way."

"Sky, I understand that. I'm not asking you to forget what Sen did. All I'm asking is that you get all of the facts before you just turn him away completely."

"He just keeps saying he never meant to hurt me."

"And I believe him. Listen you're dope. You're a good girl, you have a whole college degree, and you're from the hood. You beat the odds by attending college. That's huge. You don't think he sees the beauty and potential in you? The nigga is completely sprung over you and it ain't because you pushed out his big headed baby."

"You saying my son have a big head?"

"I'm just saying. I love my godson but let's not act like his head wasn't big as shit when you pushed him out. Nonetheless, he's here, and Sen is the father. I know how much it means to you to raise a family with both parents. This is your chance, but you have to stop holding on to anger and let him in." She voiced while I took in everything she was saying.

"What about-" I started to say, but she cut me off.

"Girl fuck Leland! No disrespect to the dead but the nigga was the ultimate fuckboy. He don't even deserve how hard you've been mourning him. He never deserved you period!"

"Lauren!"

"No Sky listen to me! I get what you've been going through because I've been going through it with you, but you can't continue to live in the past. You need to let go baby girl. You don't have to forget Leland, but if the shoe was on the other foot, the nigga would have moved on like you never even existed to him. He showed you more than enough that he did not love you the way you loved him or the way you deserved to be loved. I don't know Sen's reasons for doing what he did, and I don't want to know but I can guarantee you that had he known this was going to hurt you the way that it has he wouldn't have done it. That's just my opinion."

"I don't know girl. I just don't know. This shit is hard. Very freaking hard."

"Nothing in life that's great for us is ever easy. You are someone's mother now, and you have a man who wants to be a part of this journey with you. Let him."

"That's the thing; I'll never stop him from being a father. I told him this. It's just too much. Or maybe I'm just thinking too much. Who knows." I sighed.

"Seems to me you have a lot of thinking to do. Love when there's love to be had. That man loves you." She spoke softly.

"You tryna fix my life Iyanla?"

"Whew chileeee, I can't even fix my own life, but I know what I see. Embrace it, baby. You have everything you want at your fingertips, stop being scared."

She was right. I had everything at my fingertips but I just for the life of me couldn't grasp it. I've managed to build up a wall since he's been away and now that he's here in the flesh I wasn't sure what to do. Maybe it was time for me to embrace the cards life had dealt me.

"I gotta go, my bath water done ran cold from talking to you. Hopefully, you come around sooner than later."

"I love you best friend!"

"I love you too baby!" She blew a kiss and disconnected our call.

Sen

I was laying low since being released. I hadn't been out, just in the house chillin' tryna figure some shit out, but today I decided to slide out. It was late, maybe midnight. The streets were quiet. It was currently snowing, so everyone was probably in the crib laid up somewhere while I sat outside this house plotting.

I got word that Grimey had fucked around and caught a charge and for immunity, he gave me up. He did what bitch niggas do, but I never took him as the type. I've been rockin' with homie since we were young bulls, but he betrayed me. I would have never done no hoe shit like that to him but every nigga ain't me, and that was to be expected.

Still, there was no way I would let the goofy muthafucka live with the shit that he did. Nah. He ain't know I was out. If he did, he was just one dumb ass muthafucka because he's been posted here like he ain't have a fuckin' care in the world. I hit up V one last time to do some diggin for me about his whereabouts, and as always, she came through. So here I was preparing to handle the only problem I had left.

Speaking on V., I was proud of shorty. She had definitely changed, and I was digging it. All I ever wanted was the best for baby girl. I used to want her to get her shit together for me, for our relationship but that was the wrong reason for her to straighten up. She had to get her mind and life right for herself before she did anything for anybody else and she did that. Took some time but she did, and now she and Harmony were on their way to Texas.

Some may think she got off easy with the way she was living life, but she didn't. She hit rock bottom. It took for her to lose everything in order for her to finally see the error in her ways. Sometimes life will do that to you just to wake you the fuck up. My rock bottom was going back to jail. Remember I kept saying I felt like my time was running out? I felt that shit. I just didn't know what was gon happen.

Taking my gun off safety, I said a silent prayer before hoppin' out my whip and tuckin' the gun in my waist. Making my way to the house, my adrenaline was pumpin' something serious. I was trying to calm down a bit because I wanted to blow his mind. I was gon' act like shit was smooth between the two of us.

Knocking a few times, I waited until I heard footsteps coming to the door. I also heard a gun cock back before he asked who was it. Scary muthafucka. I don't know how I never saw how much of a bitch the nigga really was before.

"Muthafucka if you don't open up this door. It's cold as fuck out here!" I spoke loudly with a chuckle.

"Sen?" he questioned through the door.

"Fuck is you doing here so late?"

"I just got released, nigga. Slid in something warm, kicked it with my old lady and now I'm checkin on my right hand. You gon let me in or what pussy?"

"They let a real nigga out!" He smirked opening the door dapping me up before letting me in.

"Nigga you out here swole than a muthafucka huh? Ol Incredible Hulk ass."

"I see you got jokes with your Calvin from Paid in Full lookin' ass. Fuck you been up to?"

"Shit. Living. Laying low. They let you out, huh?"

"I'm here right? You know they can't hold a real nigga down." I boasted just as some chick came from the back.

"You want something to drink? Something to eat? Toya get this man something to munch on and shit!" He demanded, and I waved my hand at her to let her know I was cool.

"You sure you don't want anything?"

"I'm cool nigga. I was just coming through. You ain't reach out to a nigga while I behind the wall, so I had to come shoot the shit with ya but you kinda preoccupied. What you got planned for the week?"

"Shit. Gotta make a run to the city this Wednesday though. Tryna roll?"

"Matter of fact. We can drive my whip, I was going out there to cop some jewelry anyways. Guess I can grab it while we out there." I suggested.

"Aight cool, come scoop me in the am then. I'll be here."

"What time?"

"Like seven or somethin'. I'm tryna be in and out, feel me?"

"Yeah, say less nigga. I'll be here. I'ma go though and let you and ol' girl go back to doing y'all thang. She lookin' kinda neglected."

"Ah boy, shut yo ass up. Toya cool. She just some shorty I be bustin down from time to time. You can fuck her if you want. Bitch got a mean mouthpiece."

"Nah, I'm straight. I'll get at you though." I spoke walking out.

"Aight fam!" He called out before closing the door.

Pussy ass nigga don't even know he just escaped

death. He ain't gon be so lucky next time.

***

"What are you doing here?"

"To be honest with you, I don't even know. I just know I wanted to see you." I spoke, and after a few seconds, Skylen granted me access inside.

"You're lucky I'm up. It's Sencere's feeding time. Want to feed him?" She asked me, and I looked at her with confusion written all over my face.

"I pumped. He has milk in the bottle. I usually just give him the breast milk in a bottle during the late night feedings just to give my nipples a rest."

"Oh, I was bouta say, fuck am I supposed to do? Milk yo titty like a fuckin' cow?"

"Really Sen? That was ignorant."

"I'm just saying. I was confused. Besides, it was a joke, lighten up."

"That joke was dry as hell. Follow me." She told me, and I followed her up the stairs and into her bedroom.

"Bathroom is right across the hall, wash your hands and take off your hoodie. I don't want him to get sick. No shade or nothing."

"I understand," I replied removing my hoodie and laying it across a chair that was in the corner and walking to the bathroom.

I don't even know what possessed me into coming here honestly. I was just cruising, and she crossed my mind. I didn't think she would let me in but then again despite this hard exterior she tryna hold up she's a softy. Skylen is a complete lover.

Drying my hands, I walked back into her bedroom where she was sitting on the bed rocking him. Even though she was tired, with her hair thrown up into a messy ponytail, she didn't complain. In fact, she smiled as she looked down at him and that shit warmed my heart. "You going to stand there or come around to the other side so you can feed him, weirdo?" She asked never taking her eyes off of him. Instead of responding I went around to the other side of her bed, removed my sneakers and sat back resting against the headboard.

"Make sure you keep his head propped up and stop acting so scared."

"This shit just all new to me. You seem like you used to this shit now." I confessed as she placed him into my arms before putting the bottle into his mouth and I held it up.

"I've been doing this by myself for the past few month's, so I guess you can say that I'm used to this now. It's a routine. He wakes up around 3 am like clockwork, and I usually have his stuff ready for him. Once he's done with his bottle, I change him."

"And after that?"

"I do nothing, we just go back to sleep." She shrugged yawning.

"I can stay up with him, get you some rest."

"It's okay. I'm fine."

"Sky.. Just go to bed. I got this. It can't be too hard. I gotta burp him and shit, right?"

"Burp him and shit?" She giggled getting comfortable.

"Yes, burp him then change him."

"Aight got you. Just get some rest. You look tired."

"You sure?"

"Positive. Relax. I'm good." I confidently replied, and she just smiled watching me until she finally dozed off.

Skylen

When I woke up, Sen and baby Sen were both sound asleep, and it was the cutest thing I had ever seen. Sen had Sencere laying on his chest with his hands resting on him. Grabbing my phone, I took a quick pic of the two of them before sliding out of the bed making sure not to wake them.

Taking a quick shower, I grabbed my bathrobe and phone and headed downstairs to see what I had for breakfast. It's been a long time since I've been able to do this and for once I was well rested. Not forgetting to send the picture I had taken to Ms. Jenn I also sent one to Lauren. Unlike Ms. Jenn, I knew Lauren was up, and that was confirmed when she called me on facetime.

"Biiiiitcchhhhhhhh! Spill the tea!" She said doing the absolute most.

"I don't know what you're talking about," I responded setting my phone on the counter against my toaster.

"You lying piece of shit! What is he doing in your bed?"

"Why I gotta be all of that though?"

"Because bitch you are. Anyways what he doing over there?"

"I don't know. It's so weird. I got up to do Sencere's feeding, and there was a knock on the door. I normally wouldn't have answered, but I did, and it was him. Instead of being a bitch I let him in, and he took care of the baby for me while I slept, and I must admit it felt good to just sleep." I admitted.

"That's all that happened?"

"Duh, bitch! What else was supposed to happen?"

"Skylen.. That man has been in jail. You know good, and damn well he wants some pussy!"

"And? What does that have to do with me?"

"You the baby momma! You supposed to give him some." She stated making me laugh.

"I'm not supposed to do anything. He wants to be a father, so I'm going to let him be. Nothing more, nothing less."

"Whatever.. Admit it though, when you snapped that pic, how did it make you feel?" She questioned.

"Honestly, I'm not going to lie, it felt good seeing that. It was just cute waking up to that. It felt right too like we're supposed to be doing this whole family thing."

"Exactly. I keep trying to tell you to just let shit be. Stop living in the past friend. Let that man love you."

"Lauren, it's not that easy."

"Life ain't easy, but we survive this bitch every day. We still live it despite what type of shenanigans we have going on in our lives."

"I don't know," I told her getting the stuff together to make French Toast.

"You're going to I don't know yourself to death. You really amaze me. You have everything that you want right in front of you, but you won't reach out and take it. That shit is real baffling."

"You just don't understanddddd Laur. It's easier-"

"My bad to interrupt but you got an extra toothbrush?" Sen asked walking into the kitchen causing me to turn around and look at him.

"Yeah, uh look under the bathroom vanity, should be new ones in the bucket that's under there."

"Good lookin'!"

"Heeeeey Sen!" Lauren sung and he chuckled before speaking back.

"He still there?" She whispered.

"No bitch with you hot ass."

"Girlllllllllllll if you don't get your fucking mind together, I know something. I'm telling you right now. You don't want to be me. I've been going on these pointless ass dates just to be disappointed. I'm not winning with men or women, but here you are playing when you got a whole nigga over there tryna play house with you and y'all baby!"

"You know what? I'm sick of you. I've had enough of you today already, and it's only the morning time! Byeeee Lauren."

"Skylen, hold on. I'm only being annoying because I really want you to be happy. He makes you happy. Stop fighting it. He apologized. Stop making him pay for something he didn't do with malice. We live in a fucked-up world. People be into all types of shit, and we don't even know it. Ain't no telling what Leland was into. For all, we know there was no other solution other than death. I love you girl, I do but it's been over a year let it go. You got your answers so now it's time for you to move on. Ima let you go though. Just think about what I said. Talk to you later boo." She said then disconnected our call.

Finishing up breakfast, I heard Sencere cries and immediately ran up the stairs to grab him, but Sen had beat me to it. Standing in the doorway, I admired how attentive he was with him. I could get used to this type of scenery every day. Everything about this felt right.

"I know you're watching me," Sen spoke never taking his eyes off of baby Sen.

"I can't watch?"

"I'm not saying you can't, but you're watching me like you don't trust me."

"I've never said that."

"How didn't you? Because I had to talk you into letting me put him to sleep last night. As his father, I would never do anything to hurt him."

"I never said you would," I mumbled.

"You don't have to it's just the vibe I'm getting from you. I know I've fucked up but a nigga still a good person at the end of the day. My past isn't perfect, and I didn't have it as easy as you so I do what I gotta do to provide. That shit with ol' boy was a job a friend of mine asked me to do. Nothing more nothing less. It wasn't personal for me until I saw the look on your face when they arrested me. I can't change that shit though, it happened ma."

"Sen.. I don't want to talk about this right now. Maybe you should go."

"Nah let's talk about it. I'm tryna give you all the space you need, but that shit is becoming very hard when all I keep thinking about is you and our child. You keep acting like you're the only one affected by the things that have happened! What about me? I thought about this shit every single fucking day when I was in jail. You were carrying my seed, and not once did I see you. Not once did I hear your voice. I had to find shit out from my mom's. You don't think that shit affected me? Stop playing victim yo!" He barked with his nostrils flared, and his face screwed up.

"I couldn't talk to you! You hurt me! You hurt me Sen! Why can't you understand that?!" I shouted as my voice cracked.

"You did this!" I continued to shout making the baby cry.

This was too much. I couldn't do this. I felt like at any moment I was going to have a damn mental breakdown. My heart started beating fast, the room started spinning, and my breathing became shallow. The walls were closing in on me, and I couldn't stop them. I wanted to, but I couldn't.

Sen

"Hello, Ms. Taylor. Nice to have you back with us. How are you feeling?" the doctor spoke to Skylen.

Shorty had passed out after hyperventilating, so I rushed her ass to the emergency room. Mom dukes met us down here and took the baby home with her, so it was just me and her waiting as they prepared to run all types of tests on her.

"I feel fine now, can I go home?" She asked sitting up.

"Not so fast. We just want to run an EKG on you and give you a chest x-ray. Just to make sure there's nothing going on with your heart. I don't believe there is, but I can never be too sure."

"Trust me, doctor, I'm fine. I've just been a bit overwhelmed since I had the baby."

"I see. Any other things you've been feeling?"

"I don't know. Uh unsure of things I guess,

stressed maybe, tired. Nothing out of the norm."

"Do you have anxiety problems?"

"Not that I'm aware of."

"Hmph, we'll hold off on the testing for a second. Let me take a look at the notes the nurse wrote when they brought you in. I'll be back." He said walking out of the room that we were in.

As she sat there messing with hands and biting on her lips, I just stared at her. She was uncomfortable when she didn't have to be. Embarrassed maybe as well because she hyperventilated so bad she caused herself to pass out. The ringing of my phone caused me to take my eyes off of her briefly while I looked to see who was calling me. It was my mother.

"Sup ma?" I answered.

"Y'all still down at the hospital?"

"Yeah, waiting for the doctor to come back into the room. The baby aight?"

"He's fine. He's asleep. I was just calling to check

in and see how baby girl was doing."

"Preciate it."

"I love you, baby. Take care of her. She might not realize it, but she needs you. I'll talk to you later." She spoke before hanging up.

"Is Sencere okay?" She asked looking at me with worry.

"He's fine. Let's worry about seeing if you're okay or not, aight?"

"I'm fine Sen. I just want to go home to my baby."

"Why you keep doing that?" I asked her with my elbows resting on my knees as I looked at her. She was light weight pissing me off always referring to Sencere as her child and not ours.

"Doing what? What are you talking about?"

"Keep referring to him as your baby. He's our baby."

"He is mine!"

"So my sperm ain't help create him, huh?"

"Sen.. I'm not saying that. It's just; it's been him and I. I thought I was going to do this parenting thing alone. I was never expecting for you to come home."

"Well I'm home and we in this shit together Skylen. It ain't just you; it's us. We family."

"Okay.."

"I'm serious. Stop acting like you have to go through this shit alone. I'm here. Most niggas probably wouldn't even be dealing with all this shit, but I am, and I'm doing it because I give a fuck about you. You just need to get that shit through that thick ass skull of yours."

"Okay, I heard you the first time Sen." She snapped just as the doctor came walking back in.

"Skylen do you mind if we discuss a few things in private?" He asked, and she looked confused.

"What's wrong?"

"Do you mind if I speak in front of this young

man here?"

"Uh.. N-n-n-no I don't mind. What's wrong?"

"You were hospitalized a little over a year ago because you experienced the same thing you experienced today, do you remember having these episodes before then?"

"No, not that I can remember."

"I see. Well, I believe you may have a panic disorder, but it may have worsened since the birth of your child, so now it's a tad bit more severe. It's called Postpartum Panic Disorder. Have you ever heard of it?"

"No."

"Well, it's a panic disorder that new moms experience. Some won't but most will. It can be treated with simple lifestyle changes with how you deal with everyday stress and conflict, talking to someone like a therapist or we can give you meds. Do any of those suggestions sound appealing to you?"

"I'm not crazy!" She blurted with tear filled eyes.

"I'm not saying you are, I'm just saying you may

want to consider talking to someone. I don't want to put you on pills because let's be honest, mood stabilizers aren't the best for someone who's breastfeeding as well as active as you are. I do believe you should talk to someone. I can write you a referral to someone." He explained, but she didn't respond.

"I'll get your discharge papers ready and when you're ready to see someone have your primary doctor refer you someplace. Take care young lady." He continued to say before walking out.

Pulling my chair close to her I grabbed her hand, and she looked at me with tears in her eyes. I felt bad because before me her life probably was calm. Routined. Now she's unsure of herself, and I hated that. Her crying fucked me up inside. No lie.

I wasn't sure what I had to do, but I was going to figure it out. I wasn't giving up on us. I couldn't. I had one last problem to handle and after that Skylen and Sencere had my full attention.

***

"Sup with it?"

"Shit, it's freezing out this muthafucka!" Grimey expressed hoppin into the car.

"It's New England nigga, this shit ain't new!" I chuckled pulling off.

It was quiet for a few while I drove. He was in his phone, and I was in my head. I thought about a thousand different ways I could eliminate the nigga without it ever being traced back to me. I had just escaped a life sentence, I wasn't tryna face another one.

Merging onto the highway, I noticed a car trailing me. It looked familiar but me being the nigga that I am I wasn't worried. While I drove Sky crossed my mind. I was worried about her. I was worried about her mental. Since the hospital visit, she's been withdrawn. She had eased up on me a bit, but there was still a disconnect there.

Glancing over at this slimeball ass nigga Grimey he was smiling and shit unaware that this was going to be his last ride. Nigga had to be on his own product if he thought I didn't know he ratted me out. Muthafucka thought we were going to be on some Kum-ba-ya cool shit, but I ain't rock like that. In the streets ain't no muthafuckin snitching and if you do you gotta go. All rats must die. I lived by that.

Not being able to hold my tongue any longer I turned the radio down a bit before clearing my throat. I needed answers. I had him in a vulnerable position, so the nigga had no choice but to talk. Not that it mattered because he was gon' die regardless.

"Aye, I've been meaning to ask you something. What happened that day you were supposed to come check me?"

"What you talkin' bout?"

"The day I got arrested, nigga. Fuck happened to you?" I asked calmly.

"Ah bro I saw 5-0 and dipped. I ain't need that type of heat." He nervously chuckled.

"I feel you. I just been tryna figure out how they got my location though. Shit haven't been sitting right."

"You know the undercovers be driving

unmarked cars, shit one of em was probably tailing you."

"I understand that, but I covered all of my tracks, how they find out it was me? Only person who knew what happened that day was you, me and ol girl from the hotel."

"Fuck is you saying? You think I ratted or some shit?" He barked causing me to laugh a bit.

"I don't think you did anything," I spoke never losing my cool.

"I know you ratted. I'm just tryna figure out why."

"I'm a real ass nigga fuck I need to tell on the next muthafucka for?"

"I don't know. You tell me. Why would you have to tell on the next man?"

"I told you I ain't no snitch nigga! Take that shit up with shorty!" He said almost sounding believable.

Had Valencia not handle my problem with ol girl I probably would believe him. Shorty told everything before V slit her throat. She had no reason to lie. Grimey was just what the fuck his name said grimey. At first, I didn't want to believe that he would do some shit like that to me but he did. My own bro had set me up for his own gain since he was looking at time for some drug shit.

Getting off the highway in Whethersfield, CT. I drove until I came to this little lowkey trail named Wintergreen woods. It was a quiet ducked off place. People normally hiked here but due to the recent snow, we've had the trail had been empty. I drove here every day for the past week just to make sure that this shit would be as simple as possible.

Looking in the rearview mirror, I made sure that there was nobody coming, well aside from the car that had been tailing me this entire time. Looking over at Grimey his face held fear as well as confusion. As it should. He had no idea what was about to happen. I mean maybe he did, but he was afraid. Should've known he was pussy. In the game, death can happen at any time you just gotta be prepared for it. He wasn't.

"We grew up together. I looked at you like you were the brother I've never had, but you betrayed me. You dropped a dime on me, and I would have never done no hoe shit like that to you. I would've ate that time. Did what the fuck I had to do because I'ma solid muthafucka. But you? You's a whole bitch nigga."

"I-I-I-I-I had no choice. They ain't leave me no choice bro. You gotta believe me!"

"But you did have a choice. You did." I told him before I reached for the door handle.

"Ain't enough room in the world for the both of us. Your time's up. See you in hell muthafucka!"

As soon as those words left my lips the back-window glass shattered, and his head slumped as a bullet pierced the back of his skull. Getting out of the car I carefully opened the back door with some gloves before dousing the car with gasoline. Once that was completed, I threw a burning match on the car watching that bitch go up in flames.

"You did what you had to do baby, let's go."

Grimey was my brother. Blood couldn't have made us any thicker so knowing that he pulled that bold ass stunt had a nigga conflicted. I hate that it had to come to this, but niggas like him was all for themselves. He proved that shit, and for that, he had to go.

"I know. Shit don't hurt any less though."

"I know that's why I pulled the trigger. It hurt me to do it, but a mother does what needs to be done in order to protect her child. Let's go." My mother spoke walking away.

My OG came through like a fuckin' rider. Grimey was dead. I thought it would bring me pure satisfaction but no lie this shit kinda hurt.

Skylen

"I swear I hate this time of the year. The malls are always so fucking crowded." Lauren complained while we walked through West Farms Mall.

Christmas was just a little under a week away, and I had some last-minute shopping to do. I know Sencere won't remember Christmas but it's his first, so I was going to go all out. I had to. I also wanted to get Sen something which was why I was all the way out here.

He has been trying his hardest to get me to open up, but I was still standoffish. I wasn't sure how to get back to where we used to be. I was a different woman now. I had a baby, I was a year older, and my wants and needs had changed tremendously. When he and I first met, I was in a horrible relationship. A relationship where I questioned my worth daily. Hell, I'm still questioning myself, but the difference now is I know what I deserve, and I'm not settling for less. I just continuously question whether or not he's the guy I'm supposed to be with and will I be making a mistake by letting him in again.

As much as I tried to hate the man I couldn't. I kinda understood what he had said. I didn't approve of it whatsoever, but I understood. He simply did what he had to do. Still, something was holding me back. I didn't know if I could trust him with my heart.

"I need to go into Lord and Taylor and then Nordstrom," I spoke looking over at Lauren as I pushed baby Sen's stroller.

"For what?"

"Well I saw this cute little four-piece suit for Sencere online and I was coming to see if they had it in the store. I want him to wear it on Christmas so he can take cute little pictures. That's literally the only thing I need from Lord and Taylor."

"Nordstrom?"

"Shoes. I ordered some online, and they were shipped here. I promise after this we can go."

"Good because this mall is way too crowded. I'm

ret ta go!"

"You complain a lot, you know that?"

"I do not."

"You do. The only time you're not complaining is when you're trying to fix my life."

"Speaking of fixing your life. What's new with you and Mr. Chocolate?" She asked giggling as we walked into Lord and Taylor going straight to the baby section.

"Nothing. He's been coming around a lot, but we're still not together. If it isn't about the baby, we don't speak."

"Y'all really tryna kill me. Matter of fact it ain't even y'all. It's you. You're going to kill me. Why are you still giving this man the run around?"

"I honestly don't know. Well, I do know, kinda."

"Okay, soooo what's your reason?"

"I'm willing to let the past be the past since he's really been a great help lately but how do I know he won't hurt me?"

"You don't know. That's the beauty of it. The beauty of love. We never know how it'll turn out, but we know that it can either be a really good situation or it can be a bad one. How it turns out depends on the two people involved. Before he went to jail, you were the happiest I have ever saw you. If you loosen up a bit, I'm sure the two of you can get back to that." She spoke while I looked through the rack and found what I was looking for.

"I'm just scared. I will never forget what he did, but every time we're around each other, I can still feel the love. Maybe not love per say, but it's close enough."

"Then let go of the past and embrace your future baby. You deserve to be happy Sky."

"We'll see. We're supposed to spend Christmas together, so we'll see how this goes. You still coming for dinner and gift exchanges, right?"

"Of course! You making baked mac and cheese?"

"Yes, fat ass."

"Alright then, I'll be there. Besides, you know I wouldn't miss my baby's first Christmas. You invite your mother over?"

"I sent her a message. If she comes, she comes. If not oh well. If she does come, she has to learn how to respect Ms. Jenn, and Sen. How she spoke on Thanksgiving will not be tolerated on any level."

"Ooooh look at you standing up for ya man and ya momma in law! Go head girl!"

"Relax. I just want Christmas to be a good one and not a shit show like Thanksgiving. We're all pretty much family now."

"Yes, chile speak it into existence!" She joked.

"You play entirely too much. Let me go pay for this so we can hurry up and get home. I need to drop your crazy ass off." I giggled.

***

"Let me help you with that," Sen said walking up to my car grabbing Sencere's car seat.

"Thank you. I didn't know you were stopping

by. How long have you've been here?" I questioned grabbing the shopping bags and locking the car doors.

"About twenty minutes or so. Not long. I tried calling you, but it went straight to voicemail."

"Yeah, it died, and the port in my car blew. I've been meaning to get a new car, but I can't really afford it. I'm very frugal when it comes to money."

"Why you ain't say nothing?"

"Huh?"

"Why you ain't say nothing? I have two perfectly good cars. You can have one."

"No, I can't accept that."

"Skylen, you're the mother of my child. It's my job to make sure my child is straight, and you need a fully functioning car. If you don't want one of the cars I have, we can go look at a few. Your phone should never be dead when you have a baby. Anything can happen."

"If I tell you I'll think about it, would you drop

it?" I asked him before walking up the stairs and into my bedroom to put the bags in my closet.

"Nah," he said standing right behind me.

"Sen, you just came home from jail I can't ask or allow you to do that for me."

"You can't, or you just don't want to?"

"I'm not having this conversation right now. Where's Sencere? I need to put him to bed."

"He good. Don't worry about him."

"Sen," I said just above a whisper as he stood in my personal space.

"Why you fighting this shit?"

"I'm not fighting anything."

"You are. You're fighting what's happening naturally. I miss you." he breathed heavily as he grabbed my face bringing our lips together. Surprisingly I didn't fight it. I let it happen. Maybe because I wanted it just as much as he did.

Within minutes he had managed to get me out

of the sweater dress and leggings I was wearing as he admired my body. Since having the baby, I had gained some weight and a few stretch marks. Him staring at me made me feel a bit uncomfortable, so I tried covering myself with my hands.

"Stop!"

"Sen."

"Stop, you're beautiful." He said grabbing my hands and spinning me around and holding me from the back.

"You're so fucking beautiful. That little pudge don't mean shit to me. I like this shit." He sweet talked into my ear making me shiver a bit.

"Jensen," I moaned as soon as I felt his fingers toy with my love button.

"Oooooh yesss…"

"Pussy so fuckin' wet. You missed me? Hmm?"

"Mmmhmm…"

"Nah let me hear you say it."

"Mmmmm,"

"You miss me?"

"Oh, gawd yessss!"

"I want your juices all over my muthafuckin' hands." He taunted dipping his thick fingers in and out of my wetness.

"Bae... Oh, fuckkkkk baeeee!" I moaned louder as biting down on my lip.

"This.. feels so fuckin' goodddd!"

"You want this dick Sky? Tell me you want this dick baby,"

"Yes, I want itttt."

"Tell me what you want or I'ma stop," He spoke, but I didn't respond instead I placed my hand on top of his making him go faster.

"Fuck me. I want you to fuck meee." I moaned surprising myself.

I was real life begging this man to lay me on my bed and fuck me til I passed out. Excuse my language I wanted Sen's dick so far up in me that, that shit would be coming out of my mouth. That's how bad I wanted it. My body needed this release, and since he was here, I was going to make sure he gave it to me too.

Stopping he spun me around, so I was now facing him. With no words spoken, I slipped out of my panties and layed down on the bed. Parting my legs, I started rubbing my clit in a circular motion being sure to give him a show. Making sure to apply just enough pressure as I stimulated my sensitive spot my mouth formed the perfect 'o' as I closed my eyes enjoying the feeling I was giving myself.

Dipping two fingers into my pussy, I started fucking myself slowly imagining that it was his dick instead. Sen was a great lover. Sex with him was memorable so thinking back to the last time we were intimate wasn't hard. The image that popped up in my head made me pick up my pace and then it stopped. Not for long because soon after I felt him slide into me slowly.

"Ohhhhh," I smiled enjoying that first stroke.

"Yessssss."

"Pussy so fuckin' tight bae." He groaned just before kissing me passionately.

As our tongues did the tango, his strokes remained slow and steady like he was making love to me. I didn't mind it either because I wanted him to take his time. I wanted to enjoy the sexual bliss he was giving me. He was filling up my tiny hole with all nine inches, and I loved it.

It was such the perfect combination of pain and pleasure I was sure it couldn't get any better. Breaking our kiss, he sucked on my collarbone while my hands rubbed his head. Biting down on my bottom lip, I silently thanked God for this moment. A moment I never thought would happen again.

"I love you, Skylen Taylor. You hear me? I. Love. You." He confessed to me in between strokes, but I just continued on moaning.

Did I love him? Could I really consider what we shared as love? I know there's a connection there but is the connection deeper than the surface. Was this something I didn't want to live without? All those things were in consideration as the next set of words left my lips.

"I love you too Jensen Lewis," I spoke when he locked eyes with me, and I meant it.

I do love him. I love him with every fiber of my being. If I didn't, we wouldn't be here right now. I wouldn't have fought so hard to not forgive him. The more I tried to fight it the more the gravity of earth pulled us together. The more the universe aligned us with one another, and I was done fighting it. I wanted this man to love me. No, let me correct that, I needed this man to love me with his whole heart. I deserved that, I believe.

What started out as slow strokes had just switched to deep fast strokes and I didn't mind one bit. Thumbing my clit, he fucked me mercilessly. Sweat dripped from his chocolate skin as he never took his eyes off of me. With his eyebrows knitted and his thrusts becoming harder I knew he was well on his way to cumming. Squeezing my pelvic while he jabbed at my spot I knew it was a matter of time before I was cumming right along with him as well.

"Damn Sky, I'ma about to cum!" He grunted, so I wrapped my arms around his waist and pulled him deeper into me.

"Cum for me baby, cum for me." I cried, and he did. He came within seconds. Matter of fact we came together. As one.

After our passionate sex session, he collapsed on the side of me pulling me onto his chest. With my head resting near his heart, a tear escaped my eye. I never wanted to lose this again.

Sen

Christmas Day

"Sen, can you do me a favor?" my OG asked when I walked into her kitchen.

"Wassup?"

"You think you can carry these pans to the car for me?"

"Of course, queen."

"You nervous?"

"About what?"

"Meeting her mother."

"Lil' bit but I've had to face worse."

"I'm sure she'll like you. I did good raising you."

"You did aight."

"Boy don't you play with me. I did the damn thing as a single momma!" She boasted taking a sip of her eggnog.

"Aye ma, I never got a chance to uh, you know thank you for what you did," I told her not going into to details. We vowed to never mention how we killed Grimey together.

"No thanks needed baby."

"I hear you but I had to let you know I really appreciate you. I'ma carry these pans out to the car though, I'll be waiting outside when you're ready."

"Okay," she replied.

Putting the pans into a clothes basket, I brought them outside and placed them in the trunk neatly. Gettin' into the driver's seat, I started to hook my Bluetooth up just as in an incoming call came through. Valencia name flashed across the screen, so I answered.

"Yooo!"

"Merry Christmas Jensen!" Her and Harmony sung into the phone and a smile involuntarily crossed my face.

"Merry Christmas to you too, what y'all on?"

"Nothing, Harmony opened her gifts, and now we're watching tv. I just wanted to call and send you some cheerful greetings. Oh, anddd tell you that I saw a post that made. When were you going to tell me you were dating my friend Skylen? I saw her post a picture and because I've spent years with you, I immediately recognized who tattooed arm that was."

"You stalkin' me?" I joked.

"Not even. She's a good girl. Always has been. Treat her good. We weren't a match, but hopefully, the two of you work." She sincerely spoke.

"Oh, and another thing, I see you no longer have that problem."

"What you mean?"

"You know what I'm talking about no need for me to go into details. No leads on whoever did it."

"Ahhh, I got it. Of course not. Never leave a trace."

"Exactly! Well, I just was calling to wish you a Merry Christmas. I'll periodically check on you. Stay out of trouble!"

"It was nice hearing from you. Be good V," I told her just as my mother got into the passenger side.

"Always, talk to you soon!" She said disconnecting our call.

"Still talking to Valencia I see." She said lookng at me with side eyes.

"Nah ma, it ain't even like that. V and I ain't even on that type of time. Trust me."

"Mmmhmm sure."

"I'm serious. She finally got her shit together. I'm proud of her."

"Oh, she did huh?"

"Why you sounding all surprised?" I asked chuckling pulling off.

"That girl is a lost soul."

"We're all some lost souls to some extent. She just needed to find her purpose. I think she's good now. She ain't got no choice but to be."

"She better be because Skylen and Sencere here now. Ain't no time to revisit the past."

"You a trip, you know that?"

"I'm a woman. A smart one at that. Give her space and opportunity to come back and she will. Don't be no fool." Mom dukes preached.

I heard what she was saying and shit, but V and I were done. She knew that. She may not have been the best person in the world, but I forgave her even after everything she did. Holding ill feelings towards her wasn't gon fix shit. I had a lot of time to sit and think while I was locked up, so I knew her and I were done for a moment. She did me a couple of solid ass favors, but that was it. She had moved on with her life, and so have I.

***

Hey it's another Christmas holiday. It's a joyous thing to let the angels sing

cause we're together. We got a thing, can't let it slip away. Go outside, it's raining sleet hen our bodies meet I don't care about the weather. Let it snow.

Let it snow. Outside it's cold but the fire's blazin' so baby let it snow. Let it

snow, let it snow, let it snow.

Walking up behind Skylen I wrapped my arms around her waist while she dressed Sencere. She had put him in this velvet blue four-piece little suit which matched her blue velvet dress that fit her curves nicely. Her hair was up in that half up half down style the chicks be wearing. She was looking good. Her curves filled out the dress nicely.

"Sennnn move!" She giggled while I nibbled on her ear.

"Why I gotta move?"

"Because your mother is downstairs and my mother just texted me letting me know she's on her way."

"What that gotta do with me?"

"Everything, nasty!"

"You're so fucking beautiful. Did I ever tell you that?" I asked in her ear before releasing her and admiring her backside.

"You tell me that all the time and every time I blush harder than before." She blushed.

"Thank you."

"You don't have to thank me. I'm just happy you finally ain't being mean to a nigga."

"I was not being mean to you!"

"Shiitttttt! You were giving me the silent treatment. A woman has never ignored me as hard as you."

"Welp that just goes to show you that I'm not like other women then."

"This is true. This is very true." I told her walking around to pick up our son.

"Oh, I almost forgot. I got you something." She smiled placing a gift-wrapped box in front of me.

"You ain't have to do that ma. You done already

gave me the best gift a nigga could ever want. You gave me my son. I don't need no gift."

"Just open it Sen."

"Open mine first," I demanded reaching into my pocket and pulling out a little box.

"What, what is it?"

"Open it up and see."

"Sen.."

"Would you just open it up and see."

Listening to me she unwrapped the small box revealing a ring box. With uncertainty, she glanced at me while questioning me with her eyes. Nodding my head towards the ring box, she hesitantly opened it revealing a 1/5 silver diamond round cut promise ring. When I saw it, I immediately wanted her to have it. It wasn't an engagement ring, but hopefully one day it would be.

"A promise ring?" She questioned confused.

"Yeah. It's just something simple. I want you to

know that no matter what we go through I got you. I got us. Shit ain't going to be perfect all the time, but I just need to always understand that if you let me, I promise to never hurt you again. I promise to hold and protect your heart. I'm not turned off from a lifetime of love with you, I'm welcoming it." I sincerely spoke, and Sencere started making spit bubbles and giggling.

"I don't know what to say."

"Don't say nothing at all. Just wear it when you're ready to. Aight?"

"Okay."

"Let's go downstairs I think I hear my momma talking to someone."

"Wait what about your gift?"

"I'll open it later."

"You sure?"

"Positive. Come on." I told her, and with that, we both made our way downstairs.

"It's about time y'all brought y'all asses down the

stairs!" My mother said grabbing the baby from me while a lady who I assumed was Skylen's mother struggled with her bags. Grabbing them from her, she looked like she wanted to say somethin but relaxed and shut the door behind her.

"Hey, mama." Skylen greeted her with a kiss on the cheek.

"Hey princess." She smiled before turning to me.

"You must be the father, right?"

"Yes, ma'am I am. I'm Jensen, but you can call me Sen if you like." I introduced myself sitting the bags on the floor and extending my hand.

"Ms. Lori, it's finally nice to meet you." She spoke slapping my hand away and embracing me with a warm hug.

"It's nice to meet you as well."

"Now that we got the introductions out of the way, can we get some drinks going? I am parched!" My mother said while dancing around the kitchen with Sencere still in her arms.

"Guess that was my cue to start making drinks huh?" Skylen asked giggling.

It's always been my mother and I for holidays until Valencia came along so being here with them right now felt good. It was different because I don't have much family and the only person who ever came close to being family betrayed me, so this moment was pretty dope. Just think last year I was spending Christmas in a jail cell stressing behind a dumb ass case worrying about Skylen and her pregnancy. This year though, I was where I belonged.

I still don't know what's going on between Skylen and I, but I'm hopeful, I guess. I love shorty. I ain't ever been sure of anything in my life, but I'm sure her lil cute ass was made for me.

Skylen

I was in the kitchen putting food away and making to go plates when Lauren had joined me. Christmas was a success. My mother had been on her best behavior and even been talking to Sen. Ms. Jenn was about drunk now, so she was just being her usual self-talking shit while Sencere laughed like he understood what she was saying. Spending this time with them made me think more on Sen and I situation we currently had going on, well that and the Promise ring he had given me.

I know it isn't an engagement ring, but it's still a big deal. Like this man went out his way to look at jewelry trying to find the ring he felt was suitable for me. Just to vow that he'd never break a promise. Do you know how much thought went into that? Hood niggas ain't doing shit like this unless they really like you. He really put all of my doubts to bed when I opened that box.

Smiling to myself as I threw the aluminum pans into the garbage I couldn't help but laugh to myself thinking about how scared I was when I held the gift-wrapped box. I really thought he was going to propose. My silly ass really started stuttering because I got nervous.

"What you over there smiling about?" Lauren asked taking a seat at the kitchen table.

"Nothing." I giggled.

"It's obviously something because it got your ass over there blushing and cheesing so damn hard that I want to know what you over there thinking about."

"I just told you it was nothing."

"And you're lying, but it's cool. You don't have to tell your best friend anything. I'll just sit here and sulk in my tears since you don't care about our friendship."

"Girl!"

"It's okay. I understand. You don't have to say it. I'll just go find a new best friend."

"You are so damn dramatic!" I laughed throwing

a balled up piece of paper towel at her.

"No, I'm not. You're just being mean."

"I am not. I'm just over here smiling because this has been one of the best Christmas I've ever had. That's all."

"It has been pretty cool though. Great music, food, and my god baby looks so stinking cute in his suit. I just want to take him home wit me."

"I meannn if you want him for the night you can definitely take him."

"Why? What you tryna do? Get you some?" She inquired, and I playfully rolled my eyes before responding.

"No nasty I am not. I just need some time for myself."

"You don't have to lie. You tryna get those walls dusted off, and I don't blame you."

"Didn't I just say I just need some time to myself?"

"I heard what you said. You need time to yourself, so you can get some dick!"

"Lauren!" I damn near squealed.

"Can you shut up?!"

"It's the truth. Sky you need a good fuck session. It's been what? A year or something?" She questioned minding my business, but I didn't respond. I just walked over to the sink and started washing the dishes.

"Y'all good in here?" I heard Sen ask Lauren and I.

"We're good. Y'all need anything in there?"

"Nah, I'ma take Sencere upstairs he's fighting his sleep."

"Okay," I responded and shortly after Lauren was standing next to me but facing the opposite direction.

"What Laur?"

"What's going on with y'all?"

"Nothing. We're just.. I don't know."

"I need y'all to figure this out because y'all are seriously making my nerves bad. I promise y'all are."

"I'ma tell you something just don't scream like the damn dramatic person you are. Okay?"

"Okay.."

"I'm serious bitch!"

"Me too. Now spill it! What happened?" She asked eagerly.

"We had sex!"

"Bullshit! When?"

"The day you and I went Christmas shopping together."

"That's why you around here glowing. I knew it was something different about you. How was it?"

"I am not glowing!"

"Lie again! You are most definitely glowing. You look happy. Not to mention you've been smiling all day! I should have known it was something."

"Bitch relax. All that is not from no damn dick. You trippin'."

"I'm serious Sky. You seem a lot more calm."

"Whatever," I spoke with a shrug of my shoulders.

"Did y'all talk about anything at all?"

"What you mean?"

"Like y'all relationship. Are the two of you going to try to be in a relationship or is your dumb ass going to keep running away from real love?"

"Did you just call me dumb?"

"Yes, I did because that's how you've been acting. I keep telling you to chill out and let things happen, but noooooo you are the most stubborn individual I have ever met!"

"I am not! I'm just protecting my heart."

"From what? Love?"

"From the wrong love."

"Girl.. I don't get it. Most of us women will kill to have someone look at us the way he looks at you. You better get it together boo." She spoke before leaving me alone in the kitchen with my thoughts.

I wasn't afraid to love. I was afraid to love the wrong man again.

***

Since Christmas I had been keeping my distance from Sen. Not because I didn't want to be around him but because I needed to sort my feelings out. I needed to sit by myself and figure out if wearing this promise ring and being in an actual relationship with him was what I wanted.

So here I was on New Year's Eve sitting on my sectional nursing a glass of wine as baby Sen slept in his swinger waiting on Sen to stop by. With the ring box in my hand, I simply admired how beautiful and thoughtful it was. I can't even believe I had a child nevermind some thug ass nigga chasing behind my prude ass. I think that's what surprised me.

The two of us come from two separate worlds

but somehow managed to exist in one and produce a child. A child who we had no intentions on making. It just happened, just like everything else in life. That had to count for something, right?

Hearing the front door open, I directed my eyes in that direction, and when he came around the little corner, my heart stopped for a second. My palms became sweaty, and I started feeling all tingly inside. I was feeling like I did the first time he came over to my old apartment. Once he made it over to me, he took a seat and just looked at me.

As always he had on a Champion hoodie and sweats set with some fresh J's on his feet. His attire was appropriate for the New England weather. It was cold and snowy outside. There was a storm going on to be exact, but when I told him I wanted to see him, he came with no questions asked.

"Wassup Sky?" he asked me before licking his juicy lips.

"Nothing."

"So you called me over here for nothing?"

"Yeah. I mean no. I don't know." I said confused looking into his eyes.

"You straight?"

"Yes."

"Is it the baby?"

"No."

"Okay, I done ran outta questions."

"Sen, why me?"

"Huh?"

"Why me? Why do you want me?"

"Shit, why not you?" He asked with a shrug before placing my feet into his lap and looking at me.

"Before I met you my life was chaotic. It was wild. The way I was living wasn't safe. Shit ain't have no structure. Nothing made sense to me. But since meeting you, you've managed to add peace and value to my life. You've managed to get me to see things at a deeper level which is dope. You left an impact on me, and I didn't know how much until I was sitting up in Ludlow doing my bid. When you cut me off my energy was different. I no longer felt that peace that I did when I was around you and all I could think about was getting it back. Plus, you gave me my son. I'm forever thankful for that. I don't know what it is about you, but you're different. I like that."

"Wow.." was all that managed to leave my lips while I processed everything he was saying.

"You're a queen baby. Don't let nobody take that crown from you. I just see how beautiful you are as a person and I crave that daily. I need that. I need to be around that 25/8. I don't know how long I'ma live but what I do know is I want to be able to be in your world as long as you will allow me to, feel me?"

"Your promises.. Did you mean them?"

"Of course."

"So if I choose to slide this ring on right now, you won't break one promise that you made on

Christmas day then, right?"

"Course not. I ain't perfect or no shit like that. I can't promise to be perfect, but I can promise to try and be open to learn to love you the way you want to be loved."

Looking at him with the ring box in my hand, I took my eyes off of him while I toyed with the ring before slowly sliding it on my right-hand ring finger. I didn't know what the days ahead of us would look like, but I as dedicated to finding out. I couldn't deny it anymore. I was in love with this man. He accidentally came into my life and managed to win me over and as the clock read 11:59 pm I was excited yet nervous for the new year and the new beginnings we were going to endure.

Getting closer to him I pulled his face to mine and kissed him deeply with so much passion and intensity that you could literally feel it. This man wasn't perfect. Neither was I, but we were just the right amount of perfect for each other.

I guess I got my happy ending after all.

The End

What's meant to be will always find a way. -
Trisha Yearwood